The Mystery of The Stolen Bicycles

Collins

An imprint of HarperCollinsPublishers

Noddy and Tessie Bear were in Town Square with
Miss Pink Cat. She was telling them all about her
picnic with Mr Sparks.

"We drove all the way to Picnic Rock," said
Miss Pink Cat. "I brought five cream cakes
and Mr Sparks ate three of them!"

"I'd like to go there," said Noddy, "but I haven't enough money to buy lots of food for a picnic."

Then Tessie had an idea. "Why don't we do lots of jobs and earn some money so that *we* can go on a picnic next week?"

"That's brilliant!" replied Noddy excitedly.

Sly and Gobbo, the mischievous goblins, were
listening to Miss Pink Cat's picnic story.

"It's not fair," complained Gobbo. "We *never*
go on picnics."

"I wish *we* had a car…"
whined Sly, just as
Big-Ears cycled past.
"…or a *bicycle*!"
continued Sly.

"*Two* bicycles, you
mean," said Gobbo.
"Come on, Sly.
I've had an idea!"

Later that afternoon, Big-Ears rushed into Noddy's house.

"My bicycle has been stolen!" he cried.

"Oh no! We'd better report the theft to Mr Plod."
Noddy drove Big-Ears to the Police Station as fast as
he could.

"Mr Plod," cried Noddy, "we've come to tell you that
a bicycle has been stolen."

"I know that!" said Mr Plod, crossly. "It was stolen from right outside the Police Station!"

"But my bicycle wasn't outside the Police Station!" said Big-Ears.

"It's *my* bicycle that has gone missing!" roared Mr Plod.

"No, Mr Plod, it's *my* bicycle that has been stolen!" replied Big-Ears firmly.

"I think," said Noddy hastily, "that *two* bicycles have been stolen!"

Noddy and Big-Ears
drove all over
Toy Town.

The stolen bicycles were
nowhere to be seen.
   At Market Crescent,
Tessie Bear was selling
some cakes.

"I am having a good day," said Tessie. "I've just sold two cakes and some sandwiches to Sly and Gobbo. I've earned three coins!"

"You haven't seen two bicycles, have you?" asked Big-Ears.

Tessie Bear shook her head.

Noddy asked Dinah Doll if she had seen the
missing bicycles.

"No, Noddy," replied Dinah. "I've been very busy
on my stall. I sold Miss Pink Cat a new picnic
basket, and Sly and Gobbo some lovely green paint."

"I wonder what they wanted paint for?" said Noddy
to himself.

"Noddy!" called Big-Ears urgently. "The Skittle
children saw someone on a bicycle near
Stony Bridge!"

The two friends drove straight to
Stony Bridge.

"Look, Big-Ears!" cried
Noddy. "Bicycle tracks!"

Noddy and Big-Ears
followed the bicycle tracks all the
way to Dark Wood, but
then the tracks disappeared.

"Hmm," said Big-Ears thoughtfully.
"Let's visit Sly and Gobbo."

"What are you doing here?" Sly asked rudely as Noddy and Big-Ears drove up to the goblins' tree house.

"We're looking for two missing bicycles," answered Noddy. "Have you seen them?"

"What do they look like?" asked Gobbo, appearing from behind the tree.

"My bicycle is red," said Big-Ears.

"And Mr Plod's bicycle is blue," added Noddy.

"If we see a red bicycle or a blue bicycle," said Sly grinning, "we'll let you know!"

Noddy and Big-Ears drove back to Noddy's house.

"Those two goblins are up to something," said Big-Ears as they got out of the car.

"And I think I know what it is," said Noddy thoughtfully. "Big-Ears, let's make a surprise visit to Dark Wood tomorrow."

"I'll set my alarm clock to make sure I'm up bright and early," said Big-Ears.

Early the next day, Noddy and Big-Ears drove to Dark Wood. But they were too late! The goblins had already gone and there were no bicycles to be seen.
    But then Noddy found a clue.

"Look, Big-Ears," he said. "Bicycle tracks! And where has that green paint on your beard come from?"

"From this empty paint pot!" replied Big-Ears.

The two friends drove to the Police Station.

"Hello, Mr Plod," said Noddy. "Have you seen Sly and Gobbo today?"

"Yes," answered Mr Plod. "I went to ask them about the stolen bicycles. They were setting off on a picnic just as I arrived."

"Were they riding bicycles?" asked Noddy excitedly.

"As a matter of fact, they were," said Mr Plod, "but they were not the stolen bicycles. They were…" and he looked at his notebook…

"Goblin green!" cried Noddy. "I knew it! And now I know just where to find them!"

Noddy, Big-Ears and Mr Plod drove to Picnic Rock
and found Sly and Gobbo sitting on a picnic rug,
eating Tessie Bear's delicious sandwiches.

"You are under arrest," said Mr Plod, "for the
theft of two bicycles!"

"Prove it!" said Sly.

Noddy scraped off some of the green paint on Sly's bicycle. Underneath the green paint, the handlebars were bright orange!

"That's *my* bicycle," said Big-Ears. "I'd know it anywhere!"

"You *are* clever, Noddy!" said Big-Ears. "You've solved the mystery of the stolen bicycles!"

"I shall give you a coin for each bicycle as a reward," said Mr Plod.

"Thank you, Mr Plod," said Noddy beaming.
Now Mr Plod and Big-Ears had their bicycles
back and Noddy had enough money to go on a
picnic with Tessie Bear next week!

NODDY ™

Here are some more books for you to enjoy:

The Mystery of
The Flyaway Balloon
ISBN 0-00712359-0

The Mystery of
The Foggy Day
ISBN 0-00712360-4

The Mystery of
The Missing Friends
ISBN 0-00712358-2

For further information please contact www.NODDY.com

This edition first published in Great Britain by HarperCollins Publishers Ltd in 2002

1 3 5 7 9 10 8 6 4 2

Copyright © 2002 Enid Blyton Ltd. Enid Blyton's signature mark and the words "NODDY" and
"TOYLAND" are Registered Trade Marks of Enid Blyton Ltd.
For further information on Enid Blyton please contact www.blyton.com

ISBN: 0 00712361 2

Reproduction by Graphic Studio S.r.l. Verona
Printed in China by Jade Productions